The Secret at Jefferson's Mansion

CAPITAL 11 MYSTERIES

by Ron Roy
illustrated by Timothy Bush

A STEPPING STONE BOOK™

Random House 🏠 New York

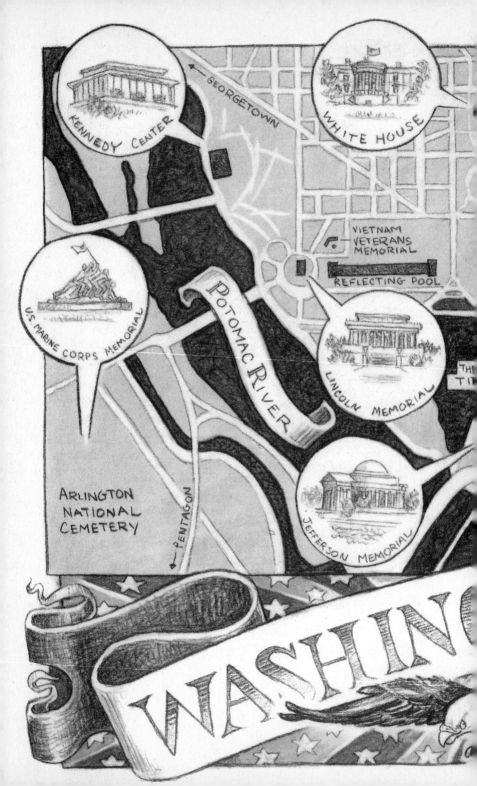

**This book is dedicated to parents and grandparents
who read to their young children —R.R.**

Photo credits: p. 88, courtesy of the Library of Congress; p. 89, courtesy of
the Thomas Jefferson Foundation/Monticello.

Text copyright © 2009 by Ron Roy
Illustrations copyright © 2009 by Timothy Bush

Published in the United States by Random House Children's Books, a division
of Random House, Inc., New York.

Random House and colophon are registered trademarks and A Stepping Stone
Book and colophon are trademarks of Random House, Inc.

Visit us on the Web!
www.steppingstonesbooks.com
www.randomhouse.com/kids

Educators and librarians, for a variety of teaching tools, visit us at
www.randomhouse.com/teachers

Library of Congress Cataloging-in-Publication Data
Roy, Ron.
The secret at Jefferson's mansion / by Ron Roy ;
illustrated by Timothy Bush. — 1st ed.
    p.   cm. — (Capital mysteries ; 11)
"Stepping Stone book."
Summary: While visiting Thomas Jefferson's home, Monticello, presidential
stepdaughter KC Corcoran and her friend Marshall investigate the theft of a
box of toy horses given to Jefferson by his grandchildren.
ISBN 978-0-375-84533-8 (pbk.) — ISBN 978-0-375-94803-9 (lib. bdg.)
[1. Mystery and detective stories. 2. Presidents—Fiction. 3. Jefferson, Thomas,
1743–1826—Fiction. 4. Monticello (Va.)—Fiction.]
I. Bush, Timothy, ill. II. Title.
PZ7.R8139Se 2009 [Fic]—dc22 2008029572

Printed in the United States of America
10 9 8 7 6 5 4 3 2 1   First Edition

Contents

1. The Hidden Cupboard   1

2. Marshall's Secret   12

3. The Key to the Case   23

4. Spike Takes a Hike   33

5. The Stranger's Face   46

6. The Figure in the Fog   58

7. The Secret in the Cemetery   70

8. Spike the Hero   82

1

The Hidden Cupboard

"Marsh, I can't see anything in here!" KC said. "Hand me the flashlight."

Marshall Li grinned. "It doesn't work," he fibbed. "The batteries must be dead. Better watch out for spiders. They love to hide in dark places."

KC backed out of her bedroom closet. "I just changed those batteries last week," she told him. She took the flashlight from Marshall and switched it on.

"Don't try to scare me," she said. "Spiders are gross, but I'm not afraid of them."

"Spiders aren't gross!" Marshall said. "They're smart and shy and wouldn't hurt a fly . . . well, maybe they would."

Marshall loved all creatures, but especially those with eight legs. He had a pet tarantula and hoped to work in the insect zoo at the Smithsonian someday.

KC Corcoran was President Zachary Thornton's stepdaughter. KC had moved into the White House when her mother and the president got married. Marshall Li, who lived nearby, was KC's best friend.

KC had decided to paint the inside of her closet, and Marshall was helping her. They piled all her clothes on KC's bed.

KC had brought cleaning rags and a stepladder from the kitchen.

"Come on, let's get started," she said to Marshall. They each grabbed a dustcloth and crowded into the closet. KC set the flashlight on top of the stepladder.

"Why isn't there a light in your closet?"

Marshall asked. "Mine at home has one."

"This is one of the oldest bedrooms in the White House," KC said. She wiped dust and cobwebs from the wall in front of her. "There was no electricity when it was built. I guess they just forgot about the closet when electricity was added to the White House."

Marshall climbed up the stepladder and aimed the flashlight around the space. He paused when it shone on one corner.

"Hey, what's that thing on the wall?" Marshall pointed to a small lump under the paint. It was perfectly round and the size of a half-dollar.

Marshall tapped the bump with the end of the flashlight. Some of the old paint flaked off. He looked at the bump more closely. "I think it's a ring," he said. He wiggled a finger under the paint and tugged. Suddenly a square piece of wall came away in his hand. He jumped off the stepladder as paint flakes fell onto his hair.

"Let me see!" KC took his place on the ladder. She shone her flashlight into a square hole in the closet wall. "It's a secret cubbyhole!" she said.

"Is there anything inside?" Marshall asked, wiping dust and paint off his shirt.

"Cobwebs," KC said. "And a couple of shelves." She stood on the top step and reached into the hole. The shelves were deep, so she had to shove her whole arm in.

KC felt a sharp edge. "I think there's something in here! It feels like some kind of box," she said.

"Maybe it's a pirate's chest filled with treasure," Marshall cracked.

"Here, take the light." KC handed the flashlight to Marshall so she'd have both hands free. She slid the thing forward and pulled it into the closet. It was a chest, but not a pirate's. About the size of a pizza box, it was made of wood and stood only six inches high.

KC set the box on top of the stepladder next to her. She wiped dust and grime off the wood.

"I wonder what's in it," Marshall whispered. He tried to lift the lid. "It won't open."

KC noticed a small round hole. "Maybe this is a lock," she said.

She thrust the chest into Marshall's arms and reached all the way into the corners of the hole. She ran her fingers across the rough wood.

"Found something," KC muttered. She brought her hand out, holding a small key.

KC's heart was beating wildly. She put the key into the small hole of the box and turned it. When he heard a click, Marshall lifted the lid.

Inside were twelve small horses. Each was about six inches long. They were different colors. Some were wooden. Some were made of clay. One was made of cardboard and twigs tied together with string. Each horse lay in its own pocket, like chocolates in a box. They looked old.

"Cool!" Marshall said.

KC wiped the inside of the box lid. "Someone wrote something here," she said.

Marshall ran his fingers over the words. "The letters are carved," he said.

THESE HORSES WERE CREATED

AND GIVEN TO ME BY MY DEAR GRANDCHILDREN.

OF ALL MY WORLDLY GOODS, THESE I TREASURE THE MOST.

Beneath the message were a signature and a date:

THOMAS JEFFERSON, 1808

"Oh my gosh!" KC said. "These horses belonged to Thomas Jefferson!"

"How'd they get stuck in this closet?" Marshall wondered out loud.

"Maybe his grandchildren put them there," KC suggested.

She gently picked up one of the clay horses. "Just think, some little kid made this about two hundred years ago," she said. "Come on, we have to show these to my mom and the president!"

KC placed the horse back in its spot,

and the kids raced down the hallway. They found the president and KC's mom in the private library, playing Scrabble. The three White House cats were each curled in a ball on the sofa.

"I don't think 'pid' is a word, dear," Lois said to KC's stepfather, the president.

"Yes, it is," President Thornton said confidently.

"Then use it in a sentence," the First Lady said. She winked at KC and Marshall.

"'Pid' is short for 'pigeon,'" the president said. "The pid flew into its nest."

"Oh, pooh," KC's mom said. "You lose a turn for trying to cheat!"

The president grinned. "Busted," he said. "What have you got there, KC?"

"Can you move the Scrabble board?" KC said.

The president slid the board to one side, and KC set the box on the table.

"We found it in KC's closet!" Marshall said. "It was hidden inside a wall."

KC opened the box, revealing the twelve little horses.

"Oh, how charming!" Lois said.

"Look what's written here!" KC said. She showed them the words Jefferson had carved into the wood.

The president read the words softly. "Amazing," he said.

Lois lifted one of the horses from its pocket. "How do you suppose these got in that closet?" she asked.

"Thomas Jefferson left the White House in 1809," President Thornton said. "I'm sure that ending his presidency and moving out was a confusing time. Imagine the servants loading all Jefferson's boxes and furniture into horse-drawn carriages. Maybe that closet just got overlooked."

KC stroked a little gray horse. "What should we do with them?" she asked.

Lois replaced the horse she'd been holding. She looked at the president. "Any ideas?"

"Yes," the president said. "These horses belong to Thomas Jefferson. They should go to his home, Monticello."

"I thought he lived in the White House," Marshall said.

"He did, for the eight years that he was president," President Thornton said. "But Monticello was his home before he became our third president. After he left the White House, he went back there to live."

"Cool," Marshall said.

"Can we take them there?" KC asked.

"I have meetings all next week," said the president. "But you kids can go with Lois."

KC's mom opened a table drawer and pulled out her calendar. She flipped over a few pages. "We can go on Wednesday," she said. "It'll be a great opportunity for you to see Monticello."

"Where is it?" Marshall asked.

"Monticello is in Virginia," the president said. "A little more than a hundred miles from here."

"I'll work it out with your parents, Marshall," Lois said. "We'll stay overnight near Monticello. It'll be a wonderful adventure. But first you have to get that closet painted!"

2
Marshall's Secret

On Wednesday morning, Marshall showed up at the White House with a bulging backpack. He set it gently on a chair in the president's kitchen. KC was finishing breakfast.

"What's in there?" KC asked Marshall. "We're only staying one night."

"I brought Spike," Marshall said.

KC almost choked on her orange juice. "You're bringing your tarantula to Monticello?"

"He likes fresh food every day," said Marshall. "And my folks won't feed him for me, so I had to bring him."

KC looked sideways at the backpack.

"Well, we can't let my mom find out," she said. "She'll freak!"

Marshall grinned and peeled a banana. "Don't worry. Tarantulas are shy," he said. "He'll just sleep the whole time."

An hour later, the kids climbed into the backseat of one of the White House cars.

The car left the city and sped past meadows, forests, and horse pastures. KC opened her book of presidents to read about Thomas Jefferson.

Marshall pulled out two jars from his pack. He had poked holes in the lids. In the larger jar, Spike the tarantula lay on a nest of wood shavings. The second jar was half filled with black crickets. They jumped around on a layer of grass that Marshall had put inside.

Before KC could say a word, Marshall

had unscrewed both jar lids. He plucked out a fat cricket and dropped it into Spike's jar. Spike grabbed the cricket with his two front legs.

"Is he eating it?" KC cried before she could stop herself.

"What have you got back there, kids?" Lois asked over her shoulder.

"Um, Marshall brought some snacks," KC said.

"Oh, goody," Lois said. "How about some for me?"

Marshall started to laugh.

"Mom, you wouldn't like them, trust me," KC said, poking Marshall.

"Arnold, have you noticed how selfish some children are?" Lois asked the driver in a loud voice. "Imagine, my own daughter won't share snacks."

Their usual driver was on vacation, so Arnold, a White House marine guard, was filling in.

"It is shocking," Arnold said, shaking his head. "Kids today."

Now KC was laughing.

"And I really could use a nice snack," KC's mom went on.

"Me too," Arnold said. "My stomach is growling."

KC and Marshall hooted with laughter as Marshall slid the jars back into his pack.

KC went back to her president book. "Marsh, there's a cemetery at Monticello!" she said. "See, here's a picture."

It was an old black-and-white photo. A high iron fence surrounded crumbling tombstones and tall trees.

"Who's buried there?" Marshall asked.

"Thomas Jefferson and a lot of his relatives," KC said. "We have to go see it!"

Marshall pointed out a sign that said THOMAS JEFFERSON'S HOME, TEN MILES. An arrow directed them onto a narrower road.

"I think I see Monticello!" KC cried after a few minutes. She leaned between her mother and Arnold.

At the top of a hill sat a brick mansion with white painted trim. Fields and gardens spread out on all sides. In the front was a wide lawn shaded by tall trees.

"We're right on time," Lois said. "I told the curator to expect us around eleven."

Arnold drove up a curving driveway. He stopped at the top and parked near a brick path. Even before they got out of the car, KC noticed a thin, gangly man hurrying toward them. He was pulling on his suit jacket as he loped over to the car.

"That must be Dr. Spender, the curator," Lois said. They all climbed out.

"Mrs. Thornton, how lovely to see you!" the man gushed. "I'm Devon Spender. We are all thrilled! The horses will make a wonderful addition to our collection. I can't wait to get my hands on them!"

KC looked at Dr. Spender. His brown eyes blinked as he spoke. Half-glasses sat on his nose. His black hair was combed straight back and he wore a blue suit that looked odd with white socks and sneakers.

KC and Marshall followed Dr. Spender and Lois up the long brick walk. Arnold came last, carrying the box of horses.

While she walked, KC took the chance to glance around. She saw a lot of big trees and gardens separated by neat white fences. Signs pointed the way to the pond, the orchard, and the cemetery.

Three people were waiting in front of the Jefferson home. "Let me introduce everyone," Dr. Spender said. "This is Mrs. Pearl Peeps, my assistant. Pearl knows all the secrets about Thomas Jefferson's years here in Monticello."

Pearl Peeps was a tiny woman with neat gray hair and very pale blue eyes. She smiled, showing small white teeth.

"And this is Mrs. Lorna Cross, our head guide," Dr. Spender went on. "Lorna is a Jefferson expert."

Lorna Cross was the opposite of Pearl Peeps. She was tall, with big hands and a thick chin. "Glad to meet you," the woman said in a deep voice.

"Finally, the man who keeps the building and its treasures safe," Dr. Spender said. "This is Mr. Gilford Tea, our security guard."

Mr. Tea had a wide face, a squashed nose, and floppy lips. KC thought he looked like a sad bulldog.

"We're happy to meet you all," KC's mom said. "This is my daughter, KC, and her friend Marshall. And this is Arnold, our driver."

"Please follow me inside," Pearl Peeps said. She led the way, and they all followed like ducklings. They walked up some steps and through a tall door.

"Welcome to Monticello's entrance hall," Dr. Spender said. "Thomas Jefferson would have greeted his guests here."

KC looked around the large room.

Every wall held something from Jefferson's life. One was covered with Native American tools, clothing, and cooking utensils.

Dr. Spender smiled at Arnold. "And are those the Jefferson horses?"

"Yes, sir," Arnold said.

Dr. Spender led them to a glass case on tall legs. "The case will be kept locked at all times," he said.

"May we see them?" Pearl Peeps asked. She nodded at the box.

Arnold carefully set the box on a table. Lois unlocked it with the key KC had found in her closet, then raised the lid.

The twelve miniature horses lay in their pockets. KC thought they looked happy to be home in Thomas Jefferson's house.

"Perfectly wonderful," Dr. Spender said, blinking. He read the words Thomas

Jefferson had carved on the box. "Thank you, Mrs. Thornton."

"Thank KC and Marshall," Lois said. "They are the little detectives who found the horses in a dusty closet."

KC and Marshall blushed.

"Well, now we must put them away for the day," Dr. Spender said. "Would you open the case, Pearl?" She did, and Dr. Spender set the box inside, leaving the lid propped up.

Dr. Spender locked the case with one of the keys on his key ring. He dropped the ring into his jacket pocket.

Mrs. Cross covered the glass case with a cloth.

"The horses will be safe here," Dr. Spender said.

3
The Key to the Case

"Would you like a short tour?" Pearl Peeps asked. "Mrs. Cross will take you around," she said. "She is a terrific guide."

"That would be lovely," Lois said.

Mrs. Peeps and Dr. Spender exited through a door on one side of the room. The sign on it said CURATOR'S OFFICE.

"Let's start in the dining room," Mrs. Cross said. She checked her watch, then led KC, Marshall, and Lois into the hallway. As they walked, a shadow on the floor under a window caught KC's eye. Outside the window, a dark figure moved quickly away.

Mrs. Cross took them to the fireplace. "Notice the narrow door on the side of the fireplace," she said. "That's a wine elevator. President Jefferson had it built so his servants could send bottles of wine from his cellar up here to the dining room."

She opened the door, and everyone peeked inside. It was a dark cupboard with one shelf big enough for several bottles of wine. "The servants raised or lowered the shelf by pulling on those ropes," Mrs. Cross explained.

"Cool!" Marshall said. "I want one in my house so my mom can send me food."

"The bedrooms are on the second floor," Mrs. Cross went on. "Normally I don't take visitors up there, but I'm breaking my rule for you!"

Upstairs, they peeked inside several open doors. Red velvet cords stretched across the doorways. Small signs said

PRIVATE—PLEASE DO NOT ENTER. The bedrooms were large and had fancy drapes over the windows.

"Which one did President Jefferson sleep in?" KC asked.

"His private rooms are downstairs, just beneath these rooms," Mrs. Cross said. "I usually save those for last."

The little group kept walking. They came to a room with children's toys in it. "His grandchildren used this as their play-room," Mrs. Cross said.

"I wonder if they made any of those horses here," KC said.

"Why, I wouldn't be a bit surprised!" Mrs. Cross said. "They also had their school lessons here. President Jefferson hired tutors for all of his grandchildren. He wrote in his diary that education was the finest gift he could ever give them."

Mrs. Cross looked at her watch again. "Now let's go back down and I'll show you President Jefferson's bedroom."

When they got to the bedroom door, everyone crowded behind the velvet rope. "The president spent most of his time in these rooms," Mrs. Cross told them. "He slept in this one, and through the arch you can see his study and book room."

KC saw an empty birdcage hanging in front of one of the windows. "Was that for a bird?" she asked Mrs. Cross.

"Yes, he had a pet mockingbird named Dick," she explained. "When he was alone, he'd open the cage and let Dick fly about. In his diary, President Jefferson wrote that Dick often sat on his shoulder and kept him company."

Marshall pointed to a fishing rod leaning in a corner of the bedroom. "Did he like to fish?" he asked.

"Indeed," Mrs. Cross said. "He said fishing helped him think. There's a little stream in the woods where he'd spend quiet moments when he had time."

"Speaking of time, I'm afraid we have to go," Lois said. "Thank you so much for showing us around this beautiful home."

Mrs. Cross made a small bow. "My pleasure," she said. She led Lois and the kids toward the front door.

"Wait, I want to say good-bye to the horses," KC said. She walked over to the glass case and pulled back the cloth.

The case was empty.

"Mom!" KC yelled. "Come here!"

Lois, Marshall, and Mrs. Cross hurried

over. They all stared at an empty case. The Jefferson horses were gone!

"Maybe Dr. Spender put them somewhere else for tonight," Mrs. Cross said. She moved quickly toward his office.

KC tried to lift the top of the glass case. "It's still locked," she said.

Dr. Spender and Mrs. Peeps came running. She was holding a pen and a notebook. He had removed his jacket and rolled up his sleeves.

They stopped abruptly at the empty glass case. "My goodness!" Dr. Spender said. He blinked several times.

"Dr. Spender, you didn't take the box out of the case?" Lois asked.

He shook his head. "Of course not!"

"Well, somebody did!" Mrs. Cross sputtered.

"But the case was locked!" Dr. Spender said. He tried to lift the top, as KC had done.

"Dr. Spender, where are your keys?" Mrs. Peeps asked.

Dr. Spender ran back to his office. He returned carrying his suit jacket. He pulled the ring of keys from his pocket. Selecting the smallest key, he unlocked the glass case and lifted the top.

"This key has not left my pocket since I locked the case a half hour ago," the curator said. Blink, blink went his eyes.

"Then someone must have another key," Lois said.

"I doubt it, but I will ask Mr. Tea," Dr. Spender said. "He's the one who gave me this key."

"Can you call him?" Lois asked.

"I'm afraid he's away," Mrs. Peeps said. "Don't you remember you asked him to buy a new lock for the basement door?"

Dr. Spender blinked. "I did? Oh well, I must have," he said. "I'll speak to Mr. Tea as soon as he returns. But now I think we should shut the building down and search every room. Mrs. Thornton, I am terribly sorry, but I promise you everything will be done to find those horses."

"I'm sure it will," Lois said. "Come on, kids, we should head over to the bed-and-breakfast."

KC stared at the empty case. It didn't seem possible, but someone had opened it and stolen the horses while they were on the tour.

"Dr. Spender, was the front door unlocked?" KC asked.

"Um, when do you mean, dear?" he said, blinking once again.

"While you and Mrs. Peeps were in your office," she said. "And when Mrs. Cross took us upstairs."

"Why, yes," Dr. Spender said. "The door is always open for guests."

"So someone could have walked in and stolen the horses!" Marshall said.

Dr. Spender blinked about ten times. "Perhaps," he muttered. "I suppose someone could have come in, lifted the cloth out of curiosity, and then—"

"But you're forgetting about the key," Mrs. Peeps said, interrupting her boss. "How could a stranger open the locked case without the key?"

4
Spike Takes a Hike

"Arnold, something awful happened!" KC cried as she jumped into the car's back-seat. "The horses got stolen!"

Arnold whipped around in the front seat. "You're kidding, right?"

KC's mom slid in next to Arnold and Marshall joined KC in the back. "No, I'm afraid it's true," Lois said. She quickly explained how the chest and the twelve horses had disappeared while they were on the tour.

"Did you see anyone enter or leave the house when you were waiting for us?" KC asked Arnold.

He shook his head. "I took a little walk

down by the woods," he said. "I sat by a stream till just a few minutes ago. All I saw were bugs and squirrels."

KC crossed her arms and slumped in the backseat. *Who had a second key?* she wondered. Dr. Spender said he got his key from the security guard, Mr. Tea. Had the guard kept a key for himself?

KC saw a streak of lightning outside the car. Seconds later, she heard the low rumble of distant thunder.

"Looks like rain," Arnold said. He craned his neck to look at the sky.

"Please take us over to the bed-and-breakfast, and then you can go back to the White House," Lois told him. "We'll call a taxi to come back here tomorrow."

Arnold started the engine and slowly drove away from Monticello.

"What's going on here tomorrow?" KC asked her mother.

"Well, I was supposed to give a speech at a little ceremony," Lois said. "One of Thomas Jefferson's relatives is coming. Turning over the horses was supposed to be a big deal." Lois sighed. "But now I don't know what will happen."

Fat raindrops splattered on the windshield, and Arnold flipped on the wipers. By the time they reached the Virginia House bed-and-breakfast, rain was falling steadily. Arnold took Lois's and KC's bags from the trunk and set them on the porch. Marshall grabbed his pack and scampered toward the porch as thunder crashed.

Arnold climbed back in the car, tooted the horn, and pulled away.

The Virginia House was a small cottage.

A low white fence surrounded the front yard. Wet rose blossoms flopped over the pickets.

Thunder boomed again as a smiling woman threw open the door. "Hello, and welcome!" she said. "I'm Norma Bates. Please come inside where it's dry."

Lois and the kids walked into a room filled with plump sofas and chairs, a fireplace, and shelves of games and books.

"I'll light a nice fire for you after you're settled," Norma Bates said. She led them upstairs to their bedrooms. Marshall had a room of his own, next to the one KC and her mom were staying in.

"You have your own bathroom," Norma told Lois and KC. "But this young man will share the one across the hall with another guest. I'll be downstairs if you need me."

"Good, now I'm going to call Zachary, then take a nap," Lois said. "Suddenly I have a terrible headache."

KC emptied her backpack onto her bed. She'd brought a change of clothes, a Swiss Army knife, and a small flashlight. For reading, she had her book of presidents and a mystery called *Danger in Deep Water.*

KC walked into the hall and knocked on Marshall's door. Suddenly the door was yanked open. "Don't move!" Marshall barked at her. "Spike got loose!"

Marshall's black tarantula zipped between KC's feet. She screeched and jumped out of the way. Spike crawled across the hallway and scurried under the bathroom door. Marshall charged after his tarantula.

KC heard Marshall talking to Spike through the door.

Then the door opened and a tall man barged out. He was wearing a T-shirt, and KC saw a tattoo on one muscled arm. He looked at KC and shook his head. "A guy can't even brush his teeth without being attacked by giant spiders," he mumbled.

The man had curly black hair and very pale skin. His eyes were the lightest blue KC had ever seen.

"Did my friend catch him?" KC asked the man.

"He'd better," the man muttered as he stomped into the room next to Marshall's.

A moment later, Marshall came out of the bathroom with Spike cupped in his hands. KC saw hairy legs wiggling between Marshall's fingers.

"How'd Spike get out of his jar?" KC asked. She followed Marshall into his room.

"I was letting him get some exercise on my bed," Marshall said. "He decided to go exploring, I guess."

"If he comes exploring in my room, you'll have to deal with my mom," KC said, trying not to smile.

"Don't worry, Spike is pretty smart," Marshall said. "He wouldn't just go up and bite someone."

KC laughed. "Too bad the guy in the bathroom didn't know that!"

Marshall grinned. "You should've seen him!" he said. "He jumped about ten feet when he noticed Spike. The guy's face turned as white as the sink and his eyes almost popped out!"

KC laughed as she pictured the man's face. Actually, there was something familiar about him. Had she seen him somewhere before?

"Let's go downstairs and play Scrabble," Marshall suggested. He dropped Spike back into his jar.

"Make sure the lid is on tight," KC said. She watched as he screwed it shut.

"Picky, picky," Marshall said.

In the living room, Marshall set up the Scrabble board while KC paced.

"I've been thinking, Marsh. What if there were two glass cases, exactly alike?" she asked. "The crook could have stolen the case with the horses in it and replaced it with an empty case. Then he wouldn't have needed the key."

"KC, the horses got taken while we

were upstairs with Mrs. Cross," Marshall reminded her. "It was only about twenty minutes. How would the crook have made the switch? Where was the other glass case hidden? And where did he hide the one with the horses in it?"

"I don't know," KC said. She threw herself into a chair. "But if the crook didn't have a key to the case, he must've done it some other way."

"Maybe it was magic," Marshall said, making his voice sound mysterious.

"Yeah, right," KC said.

"Sure," Marshall went on. "The crook was a magician like that guy on TV who makes tigers disappear. Only this guy made horses vanish!"

KC counted out seven Scrabble tiles. "I think he had a key," she said. "Dr. Spender told us the security guard might have held on to a second key."

"You think the guard stole the horses?" Marshall asked.

KC shrugged. "I don't know," she said. "But it's weird that the guard was gone while a robbery was taking place."

"Mrs. Peeps said he was doing something for Dr. Spender," Marshall reminded her.

"I remember, Marsh," KC said. "I just think it's strange, that's all."

"What's even more weird is his name," Marshall continued.

KC looked at him. "His last name is Tea."

"And his first name is Gil," Marshall said. "Gil Tea. Get it?"

"Ha, very funny," KC said.

Marshall selected his tiles. "I go first," he said.

"Why?" KC asked.

"Because I won last time, remember?" Marshall said.

"Wrong! I beat you by thirty-seven points last time!" KC said.

"Oh yeah, you're right," Marshall said.

KC stared at her tiles, but her mind was back at Monticello. Those twelve little horses had been lost for two hundred years. Would they be lost again, this time forever?

"At least we know the crook isn't Mrs. Cross," Marshall went on. "She was with us when the horses were taken."

KC thought about the time they'd spent with the tall deep-voiced woman. "I wonder why she kept checking her watch," she said.

"Let me guess," Marshall said, rolling his eyes. "To see what time it was?"

"Marsh, she peeked at her watch about ten times while we were with her," KC said. "It was almost like she was waiting for something."

5

The Stranger's Face

The rain had stopped during the night, but the morning was damp and foggy. They waited on the front porch until a green taxi pulled up to the Virginia House. Lois and KC put their bags in the trunk, but Marshall kept his pack with him.

"What're you hiding in there, Marsh?" Lois teased.

"His snacks, Mom," KC answered before Marshall had a chance.

The cab drove slowly through deep fog. "Like driving in clam chowder," the driver muttered.

He dropped them at Monticello. KC could hardly see the building through the fog. Pearl Peeps opened the door as they trooped up the brick walkway.

"Good morning, Mrs. Peeps," Lois said. "Have the detectives arrived yet?"

"I don't know about any detectives," Mrs. Peeps said. Her eyes were red, as if she'd been crying. "We had the police, though. They came yesterday right after you left and searched the house and grounds."

"Did they find the horses?" Lois asked.

"I'm afraid not," Mrs. Peeps said.

"I see," Lois said. "My husband is sending detectives from the FBI office. They should be here soon."

"The others are in the kitchen," Mrs. Peeps said.

Lois and the kids left their luggage in the hall and followed Mrs. Peeps. KC glanced at the glass case, still empty. The cloth had been taken away.

In the kitchen, a small group of people were gathered near a long table. Coffee, juice, and cookies had been set out on a red tablecloth. Dr. Spender and Mrs. Cross were talking with a tall stranger. They all held coffee mugs. The stranger was also eating a cookie.

"Ah, Mrs. Thornton, you're here," Dr. Spender said. "I wish I had some good news for you. The local police spent hours here last night, but with no luck. The Jefferson treasure has not turned up."

The stranger looked at KC, Marshall, and KC's mom. He had pale skin, green eyes, and long reddish hair tied in a ponytail. A raincoat hung over his shoulders.

"May I introduce Mr. Randolph? He

traveled all the way from Florida to see the horses," Dr. Spender said. "William, this is Mrs. Zachary Thornton, the First Lady." He nodded at KC and Marshall. "And her two children."

Marshall started to giggle, but KC nudged him.

"How do you do?" Lois said to Mr. Randolph. "Are you a relative of Thomas Jefferson?"

The man made a small bow. "Yes, his youngest daughter was my father's great-great-great-aunt."

"I'm sorry you came here for nothing, Mr. Randolph," Lois said.

"Please call me William," the man said. "It wasn't for nothing. I always like to visit Monticello."

KC thought he looked like pictures of

Jefferson she'd seen in her book. She wondered if the president's eyes had been that green.

Just then Mr. Tea walked into the room. His face was nearly the color of the tablecloth. "I'm s-sorry," he stammered. "I've searched the basement again, like you asked. I really took the place apart, Dr. Spender. The key isn't where I left it. I know it was in the drawer of my desk, but now it isn't."

"Mr. Tea keeps a small office in the basement," Dr. Spender explained. "He and I had the only keys to that locked glass case."

"So it was his key that the thief used?" Lois asked.

"Apparently," Dr. Spender said, looking embarrassed.

"But how did the thief get the key?" KC asked.

"The lock on the basement door was old and rusted," Mrs. Peeps put in. "Dr. Spender sent Mr. Tea to buy a new one yesterday. The thief must have gotten in that way and taken the key from Gil's desk."

"But how did the thief know there was a second key?" Lois asked. "Or where it was kept?"

All the adults looked at each other.

"Perhaps it was just some passing stranger after all," Dr. Spender said. "If he prowled the grounds, he might have noticed the broken padlock and gone into the basement. He might have looked through the desk, found the key, then walked into the main room upstairs and seen the glass case. It would have taken only a moment to remove the horses."

KC thought about the figure she'd glimpsed outside the window yesterday. Had it been the thief peeking at them? Or was it just Mr. Tea going about his job?

"Well, the FBI detectives should be here soon," Lois said. "Perhaps they'll have better luck sorting this out."

"Detectives?" Dr. Spender asked. "Coming here?"

"Yes, with a specially trained dog to sniff around," Lois said.

"What a great idea," Mr. Randolph said. He reached for another cookie.

"I'll excuse myself and see to that new lock," Mr. Tea said. He left the room quickly.

"Mom, can Marshall and I go exploring?" KC asked.

"Okay, but come back in an hour," Lois said.

The kids grabbed a couple of cookies, then left the kitchen.

"Where are we going?" Marshall asked when they'd closed the front door behind them. The fog was still thick near the ground, but KC could see a glimmer of blue sky.

"I want to ask Mr. Tea some questions," KC said.

"Why?" Marshall asked as he ate his cookie.

KC led Marshall around the corner of the house. She stopped next to some thick bushes. "Didn't you think that whole thing about some stranger was weird?" she asked. "Okay, maybe it was just a stranger who stole the horses. But first he had to sneak into the basement. Then he had to look in a desk and find a key. Then he had to go into the house, see the case, unlock it, and walk away with the horses. And nobody saw him all this time?"

"Well, we were upstairs, and Dr. Spender and Mrs. Peeps were in his office," Marshall said. "And we know Mr. Tea was in town. So there was no one left to see a crook sneaking in."

"But, Marsh, the crook wouldn't know there was no one around," KC said. "A stranger wouldn't know about the horses, either. Something smells funny, that's all."

They found Mr. Tea working on the basement door. He had spread a tarp on the wet ground and was kneeling on it. The old lock was on the tarp near an open tool-box. Mr. Tea was pulling a shiny new lock from its container. He held a thin screw-driver between his lips.

"Hello," KC said as she and Marshall approached the man.

Mr. Tea dipped his head and muttered something that sounded like "Hiya."

He took the screwdriver from his mouth and glanced at the kids. "They think I did it," he said.

"But you weren't here," KC said. "Dr. Spender said he sent you into town to buy that lock."

"It was Pearl Peeps who sent me, not the doc," Mr. Tea said. "So you're right, I wasn't here, but they still think I'm involved."

Mr. Tea looked KC in the eye. "I love this place, respect it," he said. "There is no way I would steal some old kiddie horses."

KC remembered something. "Were you looking through the windows yesterday around noon?" she asked.

"I've enough to do around here without peekin' in windows," the man said. "Besides, right after we locked the horses in the case, Mrs. Peeps reminded me to go into town for this lock. I stopped and had lunch with my wife before I came back."

Mr. Tea placed the new lock into the hole left by the old one. "My wife will tell you the same thing," he said. "I was ten miles away eating soup when the horses went missing."

6
The Figure in the Fog

KC and Marshall left Mr. Tea to his job. "Come on, I want to check something," KC said.

She walked around the building, stooping to look at the ground under the windows. "Yesterday I thought I saw someone looking through a window," she said. "Whoever it was would have seen us put the horses in the case."

"Well, if you're looking for the peeper's footprints, don't forget it rained last night," Marshall said. "They'd get washed away."

"Maybe not," KC said. She pointed up at the roof. "The roof overhangs the edge of the house. So the ground under it might stay dry."

KC stopped under one window next to a shrub covered with red berries. "I think this is the window in the main room," she said. Ignoring the wet grass, she got down on her knees. She moved the palm of her hand across the dirt. She felt a dent. "Look, Marsh!"

Marshall knelt down, too. "What am I looking at?" he asked.

"The ground is flat here, like someone walked on it," KC said. "But look at this."

She put her fingers in two deeper dents, closer to the building. "I think these holes were made by someone up on tiptoes," she said. "The windows are high, so anyone looking in would have to stand on his toes!"

"You could be right," Marshall said.

"But whose feet are they, and what was he looking at?"

"That's what we have to find out," KC said. She stood up and walked to the other side of the bush. Behind it, a door was partly covered with branches.

"I wonder where this goes," KC said.

"I bet we're about to find out," Marshall said.

Marshall held the branches back while KC grabbed the black door handle and tugged. It opened to a set of stone steps leading down into darkness.

"Where's your flashlight?" Marshall asked. His voice sounded hollow.

"Upstairs in my backpack," KC said. "Leave the door open so we can see."

She started down the stairs, and Marshall followed. On the third stair KC kicked something. It clattered down the steps.

"What was that?" Marshall asked.

"Something shiny," KC said. She made her way to the bottom of the steps and groped around. "Found it!" she said.

It was a flashlight. KC clicked it on.

"Who would leave a flashlight here?" Marshall asked.

"Good question," KC said. "But I'm happy they did." She moved the light's beam around. They were in a small room. The floor was packed dirt, and old wooden shelves filled three of the walls.

"Are those wine bottles?" Marshall asked. He picked up an empty, dusty bottle and sneezed.

Suddenly the cellar door slammed.

"What happened?" KC asked.

Marshall ran up the steps and tried to shove the door open. It wouldn't budge. "We're locked in!" he said.

"Maybe there's another door." KC shone the flashlight around the room. She saw only crumbling shelves and cobwebs. Then she noticed something else. Two of the shelves were missing. In their place was a narrow door. "Look, Marsh," she said, pointing the flashlight beam.

Marshall hurried over and pulled the door open by its small round handle.

"It's the wine elevator!" KC said. "We must be right under the dining room."

"We can yell and someone will hear us!" Marshall said.

"No, wait a minute!" KC said. She lowered her voice. "Whoever locked us in might be up there."

KC shone the light on the shelf inside the little elevator. She touched the ropes. "Marsh, why is the elevator down here?" she asked. "When Mrs. Cross showed it to us yesterday, it was upstairs."

"Someone must've sent it down," Marshall said. "KC, the horses!"

"What are you talking about?" KC asked.

"I think the crook sent the horses down in this elevator!" Marshall said. "Whoever took the horses out of the case had to hide them fast, so he lowered them down to the basement."

"Why do that?" KC asked. "Why not just walk out the front door with them?"

"Someone might be coming in and see him," Marshall answered. "Or her. The question is, where are the horses now?"

KC aimed her flashlight beam at the old dusty walls. "The thief must have taken the chest out of here and hidden it somewhere else."

"Right, because he knew the cops would search the building!" Marshall said.

"And whoever it was probably locked us in here," KC said.

"So what do we do now?" Marshall asked. "Wait till your mom misses us?"

"No, she won't worry for at least an hour," KC said. "And I sure don't want to stay here that long!"

KC stepped closer to the wine elevator. She studied the shelf and the ropes. "Marsh, do you think you could pull me up if I squeeze into this thing?" she asked.

"What?" he squeaked. "And leave me here?"

"Only for a minute," she said. "I'll come back and unlock the door."

"What if the bad guy sees you?" Marshall asked.

"If I see anyone, I won't say that we got locked in," KC said. "I'll just pretend I'm fooling around with the wine elevator. You know kids, always getting into mischief!"

"Can you fit in there?" Marshall asked.

KC handed him the flashlight. Then she folded herself onto the little shelf. "Now try to haul me up. It's only about ten feet."

Marshall set the flashlight on a shelf, grabbed the ropes, and gave a yank.

KC moved up about a foot.

"Hey, it's easy," Marshall said. "Jefferson did something to make it real light."

"Okay, pull me all the way up," KC said. "And don't let go until you feel me get out in the dining room. I'll be back soon."

Marshall pulled on the ropes and KC slowly rose inside the wine elevator. Suddenly it was dark. She could see nothing. But she heard her own breathing, the whisper of the ropes, and the squeak of the shelf.

After a moment she bumped her head lightly. She had reached the top. She put her ear against the inside of the little door. She couldn't hear any voices, so she gently pushed the door open.

The dining room was empty. KC untangled her legs and stepped out of the elevator. She dashed out the front door and raced around the side of the house.

KC saw how the door had been locked. Someone had wedged a screwdriver under the handle. KC knew she had seen other

screwdrivers like it in Mr. Tea's toolbox!

She pulled out the screwdriver and yanked the door open. Marshall almost fell on her. "What took you so long!" he said.

"Why?" KC asked. "Did a spider scare you?"

"Ha!" Marshall said.

Just then they heard a car engine on the other side of the building. A car door slammed. Then a dog barked.

"That must be the detectives!" Marshall said. "I never met an FBI dog before."

Before either kid could move, a figure came out from behind the building. The figure was tall, moving fast toward the thick woods, and draped in a long coat. KC couldn't see the face because of the fog. She couldn't even tell if it was a man or a woman.

"Come on, Marsh!" KC whispered. She grabbed Marshall's arm and dragged him toward the woods. A wide path led through the trees. Parts of it were covered in pine needles, but in most places it was raw mud.

Even with the fog, it was easy to see deep footprints. The kids hurried, following the tracks in the mud.

KC almost stepped on something furry on the ground. She picked up a wet, muddy wig and showed it to Marshall. "Recognize this?" she asked.

Marshall shook his head.

"William Randolph was wearing it an hour ago," KC said. Suddenly she knew exactly where she had seen this Mr. Randolph before. And it wasn't in her book of presidents!

7

The Secret in the Cemetery

"What's going on?" Marshall whispered. "Why was he wearing a wig?"

"I'll tell you later," KC said. "Come on!"

KC and Marshall jogged along the muddy path. The fog was as thick in the woods as on the lawn. At times, it was like running through clouds. Then the path got wider. Someone had planted shrubs and covered the path with shredded pine chips.

Marshall grabbed KC by the arm. "Check it out!" he whispered.

Straight ahead of them was a high black fence. Through the rails KC and Marshall saw tombstones. Fog clung to the stones.

"It's Jefferson's cemetery!" KC whispered.

"Let's follow the fence and see if we can find a way to get in. Stay in the bushes if you can."

"Get in? Who wants to get in?" Marshall moaned.

"We do," KC said. "I think William Randolph stole the horses and hid them in the cemetery. He must've thought no one would look here. But now that the detectives and their dog are here, he came to get them!"

Before long they came to a gate. The bars were thick black iron with spikes on the top. There was a padlock hanging from a chain, but it was unlocked. KC pushed the gate open. She prayed it wouldn't squeak.

It didn't. The kids crept through the gate. Suddenly KC stopped. She put her mouth to Marshall's ear. "Listen!" Then she pointed to their right.

A figure was crouched under a tree. KC heard clinking and thunking noises and realized the figure had a shovel. He was digging.

"Oh gosh, it's a grave robber!" Marshall whimpered.

"No, it's William Randolph, horse thief," KC said.

Holding her breath, KC inched closer. She drew Marshall behind a tall tombstone.

The noises stopped. KC peeked from behind the grave marker. Randolph was holding the chest of horses. He wiped it off with the sleeve of his raincoat.

They watched him pull a cell phone out of his pocket. His voice carried easily. "Hello, Yellow Cab?" he said. "Pick me up on the road below Monticello. A big tip if you get here in five minutes! I'm going to the Virginia House bed-and-breakfast."

The man turned and jogged toward the gate. KC and Marshall were well hidden behind the tombstone. When they could no longer hear his footsteps, they started after him.

"Why is he going there?" Marshall asked. "I don't get it."

"Marsh, remember when Spike ran into the bathroom yesterday?" KC asked.

"Yeah," Marshall said. "Some guy in there nearly had a heart attack!"

"That guy is William Randolph, the crook!" KC said. "He looks different because he disguised himself as a relative of Thomas Jefferson."

"But who is he really? How did he even

know about the horses?" Marshall asked.

"I'm not sure," KC said. "But now we have to tell the detectives where he's going. Come on!"

The kids raced back along the path, keeping an eye out for the thief. KC figured he had cut through the woods so he'd come out on the main road.

She and Marshall ran faster. They were out of breath as they reached the front door of Monticello.

"KC! Where have you been?"

KC stopped and whipped around at her mother's voice. Lois was sitting in a shiny black car with Arnold. Two other cars were parked nearby.

"Mom, we found the crook who stole the horses!" KC yelled as she cut across the lawn toward the car.

KC jumped into the backseat and held the door for Marshall. "Arnold, we have to go back to the bed-and-breakfast!" she cried. "Please, he has the horses with him and he's getting away!"

Lois turned to Arnold. "Do it," she said.

Arnold gunned the engine and tore out of the driveway. He drove as fast as he could down the long, winding road.

Her mother turned around. "Okay, I'm listening," she said. "And why are your clothes filthy? And your hair! You look like you've been living in the forest!"

"Mom, that man who said he was William Randolph? He's a fake!" KC gushed. "He stole the horses and he's getting a cab back to the Bates place!"

"Tell me later," Lois said. "Arnold, can't you go any faster?"

With a squeal of the tires, Arnold roared onto the town road. He leaned on his horn and sped past slower cars. Finally he braked to a stop in front of the Virginia House.

Before anyone could get out, a cab pulled up behind them. The man who called himself William Randolph jumped out. He was clutching the box of horses to his chest. Without even glancing at the black car, he raced up the steps and through the door.

Lois handed KC her cell phone and a slip of paper. "Honey, call the detectives at Monticello!" she said. "Tell Agent Blake what you told us! Arnold, come with me."

Lois and Arnold ran into the bed-and-breakfast.

KC dialed the number and quickly told

Agent Nancy Blake what had happened. Then she opened the car door. "Come on, Marshall. I don't want to miss this!" They dashed up the front steps.

When KC opened the door, she saw William Randolph lying facedown on the floor. Arnold was sitting on him. Arnold's belt was wrapped around the man's ankles. His Marine Corps necktie made nice handcuffs.

Lois was on the phone in the corner. Mrs. Bates stood behind her desk, guarding the twelve little horses.

"Get off me, you overgrown Boy Scout!" the man shouted at Arnold. "You can't prove nothin'! I found those horses, and you can't prove I didn't!"

"I can prove it," KC said. "Your fingerprints will be on the chest, the shovel, and the key you used to unlock the glass case."

The man glared at KC. His face was red, but he grinned. "The key, huh? And how was I supposed to get the key, Miss Know-It-All?" he spat.

Lois was off the phone. She came and put her arms around KC.

"Your mother gave the key to you yesterday," KC said. "After she stole it from Mr. Tea's desk."

"You don't know nothin' about my mother," the man on the floor said.

"She's Mrs. Peeps," KC said. "You two have identical eyes. Yesterday you watched us through the window and waited till no one was around. Then you snuck in and used the key to open the case. You took the chest and lowered it to the wine cellar on that little elevator."

The man blinked at KC. Then his face dropped to the floor. He stopped struggling with Arnold.

"Your green eyes are really green contact lenses, aren't they?" Marshall asked.

The man didn't answer.

"You forgot your flashlight in the wine cellar, which helped us escape," KC said.

"It was pretty rotten to lock us down there," Marshall said.

"I didn't lock you in nowhere," Arnold's captive said. "Blame that on someone else."

The front door burst open. Two FBI detectives crowded into the room. The female detective walked over to Arnold. "Want to tell me who this is?" she asked, pointing to the man under Arnold.

"Thank you for coming so quickly, Agent Blake," Lois said. "This man on the floor is Mr. Peeps. He and his mother stole the Jefferson horses. I'll explain the rest on the way to Monticello."

Agent Blake snapped her handcuffs on Mr. Peeps's wrists. Arnold's belt and tie were returned to him. KC and Marshall went back to Monticello with Arnold. Lois rode with the other detective.

The five of them hurried up the brick walkway once more. Arnold carried the chest of horses.

"You'll be arresting Mrs. Peeps," Lois told the other detective.

"How will I know her?" he asked.

"She has pale blue eyes," KC said. "Just like her son."

8
Spike the Hero

That night, KC and Marshall sat with KC's mother and the president, sharing a pizza.

"So it was the blue eyes that tipped you off?" the president asked KC.

"Yes, but at first I believed there were two different men," KC said. "The guy we saw at the bed-and-breakfast didn't look anything like William Randolph at Monticello."

"That's because he was wearing a wig and green contacts," Marshall added. "I think Spike knew he was a crook. That's why Spike went into the bathroom after the guy!"

"Spike? Bathroom? What do you mean, Marshall?" Lois asked.

"That's a whole other story!" KC said.

Marshall burst out laughing.

"It seems that Mr. Peeps has been in a Florida prison," Lois said. "When he got out, his mother brought him to Monticello. After I telephoned about the horses, they hatched their plan. The Randolph disguise was so he'd have a reason to be in the building."

"Mrs. Peeps is the one who told Mrs. Cross to take us on a tour," KC said. "She also sent Mr. Tea to town, to make sure no one would see her son steal the horses."

Marshall looked at KC. "Did he lock us in the cellar?" he asked.

"No, that was Mr. Tea," Lois said. "He saw the door ajar and closed it with his screwdriver. He had no idea you kids were down there."

"The whole place needs a new security system," the president said. "I've made arrangements to have it done, and Mr. Tea will be in charge. I think Thomas Jefferson would be pleased."

KC yawned. "I'm going to bed," she said. "Marsh, can you stay over?"

"Sure, if it's okay with my folks," said Marshall.

Lois began cleaning up the pizza scraps. "I've already called your parents," she said. "Sweet dreams, you two."

"Nighty-night," President Thornton said. "Don't let the bedbugs bite."

The kids walked down the hallway to their bedrooms. Marshall was carrying his backpack. "I hope Spike doesn't decide to go for one of his walks tonight," KC said. "You'd never find him in the White House."

"Don't worry, he's sound asleep," said Marshall, patting the pack.

They said good night, and KC walked into her bedroom. When she opened her closet door, she could still smell the fresh paint. She had left the hidden cupboard uncovered. It was a perfect place to keep her diary and piggy bank.

KC changed into her pajamas and pulled back the covers on her bed. She jumped backward. A cardboard cutout of a big black tarantula sat on her pillow. Right away KC knew Marshall was the culprit.

KC grabbed her flashlight and tiptoed down the hall to Marshall's bedroom. She tapped lightly on the door. When he didn't

answer, she stepped quietly into his room.

Marshall was sound asleep in his bed. On his nightstand stood Spike's jar. But that was not what KC had come looking for.

She shone her light around the room. There it was! The jar of crickets sat on the windowsill.

KC picked up the jar and twisted off the lid. Then she tiptoed over to the foot of Marshall's bed. She lifted his blanket and slid the opened cricket jar next to his bare feet.

Back in her own room, KC snuggled down into her bedcovers. She hoped she'd stay awake long enough to hear Marshall's scream.

Did you know?

Did you know that Thomas Jefferson designed Monticello himself? He loved his mansion in Virginia, and even when he was president, he spent a lot of time there.

Jefferson wanted to have all of the most modern inventions at his home. Many of his gadgets at Monticello were still very rare in America at the time. He installed a wine elevator, which KC and Marshall discovered (though KC is too big to fit in the real one!). The weather vane outside connected to an indoor compass so that people could see which way the wind was blowing without leaving the building.

Thomas Jefferson loved vegetables. He kept a detailed journal of his gardens at Monticello and liked to experiment with growing vegetables from other countries. He was one of the first people to grow tomatoes in the States.

In the entrance hall is Jefferson's Great Clock, another of his own designs. It had to be wound only once a week and was powered by two enormous weights on either side. When it was being put into place, Jefferson realized that the weights were much longer than the height of the hall. He decided to let the weights hang through holes in the floor. The face of the clock is at the top of the hall—but the weights are in the basement!

Help Dink, Josh, and Ruth Rose . . .

. . . solve mysteries
from A to Z!